I0640942

Firebrand

Firestorm

The Ancestors of Bjorn Esterday

Volume 03

Encounters

1770 & March 1776

Wynter Sommers

Wynter Sommers

This work is registered with the UK Copyright Service, in
accordance with the Copyright, Designs and Patents Act 1988
All rights reserved 284718040

USA Copyright © 2015 GJ dePillis
© 2015, TXu001966602 / 2015-05-08 and TXu001983965 / 2015-11-04

Library of Congress Control Number: 2020943167

Published by Pure Force Enterprises, Inc.
California, USA
Since 2002

INGRAM

INGRAM® Distribution

ISBN-13: 978-1-7184-0015-3
ISBN-10: 1-7184-0015-2

DEDICATION

To those who feel strongly about truth,
justice, and the integrity of America;
your honorable actions make us proud.
To those who wonder if their daily
choices matter; your small decisions
impact generations to come.
To those everyday people who don't think
they have what it takes; when you strive
for extraordinary things, the impossible
becomes reality.
Your dreams today become our future
tomorrow.
Thank you for everything you do.

Bjorn Esterday
Was Not Born Yesterday
Series

Firebrand (15 Volumes+Conversation Station Book)
Edges (9 Stories +Conversation Station Book)
Gone (18 Stories + Conversation Station Book)

Bjorn EDGES Series
EDGES Book 1-Swift Encounter
EDGES Book 2-Rousing Attack
EDGES Book 3-One Foot Under
EDGES Book 4-Earthshake
EDGES Book 5-Broken String
EDGES Book 6-Key Witness
EDGES Book 7-Who is She?
EDGES Book 8-Vanish
EDGES Book 9-Chase or Die

Bjorn Series Alternate Reading Plan

1st	Edges Book 1		22nd	Gone Book 10
2nd	Edges Book 2		23rd	Firebrand Vol 9
3rd	Gone Book 1		24rd	Gone Book 11
4th	Firebrand Vol 1		25th	Firebrand Vol 10
5th	Edges Book 3		26th	Gone Book 12
6th	Firebrand Vol 2		27th	Gone Book 13
7th	Gone Book 2		28th	Firebrand Vol 11
8th	Gone Book 3		29th	Gone Book 14
9th	Firebrand Vol 3		30th	Firebrand Vol 12
10th	Gone Book 4		31st	Gone Book 15
11th	Firebrand Vol 4		32nd	Firebrand Vol 13
12th	Gone Book 5		33rd	Gone Book 16
13th	Gone Book 6		34th	Firebrand Vol 14
14th	Edges Book 4		35th	Gone Book 17
15th	Firebrand Vol 5		36th	Firebrand Vol15 (End)
16th	Gone Book 7		37th	Gone Book 18 (End)
17th	Firebrand Vol 6		38th	Edges Book 5
18th	Gone Book 8		39th	Edges Book 6
19th	Firebrand Vol 7		40th	Edges Book 7
20th	Gone Book 9		41st	Edges Book 8
21st	Firebrand Vol 8		42nd	Edges Book 9(End)

ACKNOWLEDGMENTS

We acknowledge those who actively build peace. We acknowledge all the selfless talent which contributed to creating meaningful tokens of consideration and sharing. We acknowledge that every person has a daily choice of right or wrong... and we thank you for choosing the right, good, honorable path filled with integrity because that is the difficult and brave path. Small choices today become lasting monuments of loving hope tomorrow.

CONTENTS

0 PREFACE

Last time, we saw Jane and Polly experience their own struggles. Each, at the time, may have felt totally alone, assuming nobody could understand their stresses. If they had known of the existence of the other, they may have even preferred to swap places.

Yet, as in modern times, each of us experience struggles and yearn to be in another situation, not realizing the full load of stresses involved in walking in another's shoes.

Instead of yearning to be elsewhere, focus on handling your task at hand. Instead of running away from something; charge into the thick of the figurative conflict with a strategic battle plan and conquer your own fears.

As Polly searches for hope and Jane searches for justice, understand what you search for and then look around and see if you can help another reach their goal. Sometimes it is by helping another that you will reach your own goal.

.

1 CHAPTER 19: (MARCH 1776) Billy Dawes Stops the Carriage

Billy Dawes halted the carriage. It was at a complete stop in the middle of the road. No other signs of horses or carriages were about at this still dark, early morning hour.

Jane thumped the roof of her carriage

urging the driver of the carriage to continue riding onward.

Yet, Billy Dawes did not respond as Jane would have expected. There was no response at all. It was as if he were no longer on his perch.

Jane glanced at Silversmith and then the carriage door to indicate that Silversmith should investigate. Jane was perplexed and a tad perturbed at this change in plans.

Understanding this non-verbal instruction, Silversmith pulled her cloak a bit tighter to brace against the cool air. Her hand hesitated at the door, then Silversmith glanced back at Jane as if to confirm if this was what she really wanted.

Jane nodded and Silversmith opened the door and, without stepping onto the ground, she leaned her weight on the door and stood up, craning her neck to locate the driver.

Quickly, Silversmith swung herself back into the cabin.

"He's not there, Miss Jane. Mr. Dawes is not sitting where he should on the perch."

"Well, perhaps he needs your assistance. You should find where he's gone. "

"But, Miss Jane…" Silversmith protested, "What if he requires… some private time…"

"Silversmith, if that were the case, he'd have been back by now."

"What if he encountered a disagreeable situation?" Silversmith pressed.

"Then, I think he would appreciate your assistance." Jane replied. Then, understanding Silversmith's reluctance added, "Listen, Silversmith," Jane started kindly, "Remember when we heard in town about Captain Preston?"

"No, Miss Jane," Silversmith responded with wide eyes.

"You remember... he fought the Concord fight bravely. He was also involved in that Boston incident that Magistrate Pinkney told us about before he took Uncle Floyd's body away. Well, I read that Captain Preston carried with him what he considered 'the basics'. The Bible, the Catechism, Watt's psalms, hymns and perhaps an almanac or two."

Silversmith replied, "I packed those things. The Bible and Watt's psalms."

"There you have it, then," Jane smiled, "We have the same tools and must be just as brave Captain Preston. Now, off you go... find our Mr. Dawes so he may resume driving those horses."

Silversmith took a deep breath to fortify herself with renewed energy and then with determined bravery, she stepped down, holding the carriage door. On the road, she closed the door securely behind her to protect her mistress. Then Silversmith moved cautiously off into the darkness.

Things were quiet.

Jane peered out, but it was so dark. Only the stars in the sky were beginning to fade as they succumbed to the break of early dawn. Still, it was not enough light for Jane to see what was going on.

But a moment later, Silversmith came rushing back and flung open the door.

"You were right, Miss Jane," the out-of-breath Silversmith stated matter-of-factly with a perplexed look on her face. "Our driver, Mr. Dawes, does need help, but if you'll pardon me, Miss Jane. I think he may need your assistance, as well."

2 CHAPTER 20: (MARCH 1776) Button and Day Three With the Tribe

Button was now re-evaluating his love of nature and his choice to be isolated from their closest neighbor. While continuing the trek with his Indian captors, Button wondered that if he did live near a neighbor, would they have been able to unite and fight these attackers? Or would they simply have become yet additional prisoners.

Well, no matter, now, Button thought.

He was the only prisoner still, remaining in step with his two guards.

He determined that if they pinned him in a blanket again, he would be fitful so they could not sleep. For this plan to work, Button knew that during waking hours, he must be very compliant, helpful, and appear to enjoy this new role, his captors had foisted upon him. Button turned to the men walking on either side of him and smiled at each one.

They paused at a stream and his captors caught a large fish.

Now being familiar with how to prepare it, Button scooped up clay mud from the bank of the stream and patted a portion of mud into an oval shape, while his captor took a flint knife and gutted the fish before handing it back to Button.

Button took the fish and laid it on the flattened clay disc, while he scooped up some more clay and patted it down, placing it on top of the fish and pinching the edges like the dough one places on top of a pie.

The fish were abundant in this stream. That was good.

The more the men ate, the more sleepy they would be.

The Indian with the knife took a break and laid it down on the bank while he washed his hands. Slowly Button reached for the knife, hoping he could stash it away before the man noticed it missing.

As Button picked it up, the man turned around and looked at Button, pausing. Button, now abandoning his original plans, smiled and handed the flint knife back to its owner. Button pointed to the stream, where luckily another fish swam within reach. Thinking Button was asking to catch more fish, the man stabbed it with a stick and handed the wiggling creature to Button, who took it off the stick and laid it on the bank for the man to gut.

Yes, Button's plan to steal away a knife or some weapon, had to be abandoned.

Once Button made a few of these clay pies filled with fish, he gathered wood branches and piled them up. One of the fellows smacked two rocks together to cause a spark and started a fire. Then, Button placed the clay pies onto the fire, poking them with a stick until the clay hardened.

Just as on the previous night, once the clay was hard, the items were removed from the fire, allowed to cool, and cracked open so the scales of the fish stuck to the sides of the clay.

Fragrant steam wafted out from each pie and every captor fed himself until satisfied. Button urged each man to eat, even foregoing a portion he should have taken for himself. When one captor looked full, Button would crack open another clay disc handing it to the man.

Button happily started to clean up, as he was instructed the day before. The men did not interfere, so Button assumed this was what they were hoping for, a malleable willing servant. The others rubbed the oils from the meal into their skin and then laid out blankets for the night.

When his two guards yawned, Button was satisfied that he was successful in disrupting their sleep the night before. He determined to do so this evening, as well.

Again, he laid down obediently while a blanket was placed over him. This time, instead of laying flat, Button bunched his knees so when the men would recline next to him, they would not be as close. Again, the same two men lay on either side of Button, pinning him down.

He waited.

The men next to him started to snore. Soon, the others emitted rhythmic breathing sounds of a deep slumber. Button laid there, looking up at the stars. How many days of walking awaited him?

Would they be at their destination tomorrow after three full days? This was reasonable to assume.

Waiting another day might be too late. Then again, he did witness one of the men shooting a bird with a bow and arrow. If Button ran, that man could easily shoot Button down. The man who cut the fish, would probably scalp him. Perhaps he would bring them more money as a living slave instead of being a scalped corpse, but... Button didn't know what to do.

He lay very still.

Carefully, he straightened his knees, giving him a bit of a gap underneath the blankets.

He turned his palms downward and slowly pushed to see if he could inch his body out of this cocoon.

Bit by bit, Button moved, but when one of the men in camp stirred, Button froze and forced himself to breath deeply to imitate the sounds of sleep.

Finally, Button slipped out of his blanket and stepped away from his sleeping captors.

He stood and stepped backwards, ready to pivot and run, but a dry leaf cracked under his foot. One of his sleeping guards stirred

.

3 CHAPTER 21: (MARCH 1776) BaCoun?

Jane furrowed her brow as she looked up into the dark early morning sky. Jane peered at Silversmith, who stood outside the carriage in the brisk air. She extended an arm to help Miss Jane step out onto the deserted road.

Apparently, Jane was to come to the aid of her new driver, Mr. Dawes with...well...some such matter.

Jane wished she would have carriage steps to ease her descent, but they were packed away up where the driver should have been. Silversmith probably didn't know where they were.

Jane understood she would have to make some sacrifices during this undertaking and was determined to accepted the difficulty before her with grace.

With a deep breath, Jane hopped down from the comfortable carriage to the dirt road below. When she landed with bent knees, Silversmith had to catch her arm to make sure Jane didn't tip over. Once upright and confident she was now on *terra firma*, Jane noticed her hem had become dusty.

Jane uttered a soft groan. Oh, how she hated having to walk around town in old fashions and a make- shift pannier, but now she would arrive as a guest to an estate wearing a dirty dress?

She started to smooth her skirts in

annoyance, and fluffed her home-made *pannier* so her silhouette was proper once more. Then, she forced a smile as she realized she would not make one friend here in these colonies. She would have to be content being a solitary spinster.

She forced a smile at Silversmith. "Thank you for assistance, Silversmith. Now where is this supposedly reliable Mr. Dawes?"

"Follow me," Silversmith guided as she stepped away, then Silversmith continued, "Mr. Dawes stopped because he saw something which he felt he needed to investigate."

"Well, I have my own investigation I must conduct and I will inform Mr. Dawes of that once we find him," Jane replied curtly.

As Jane and Silversmith neared the shadowy silhouette of Mr. Dawes, Jane noticed he was not alone. "Who is with him, Silversmith?" Jane asked cautiously.

But, before she could answer, the second person presented herself to the trio. Before all of them was a blood-splattered wounded woman who seemed barely conscious on the ground. Mr. Dawes was attempting to revive her.

Billy Dawes turned to Silversmith and Jane. "I almost missed seeing her, but felt it was my duty to come to the aid of a colonists in distress."

Jane, now ashamed at the thoughts she had recently harbored replied, "Indeed, Mr. Dawes you were right. This woman has suffered a great ordeal."

"Her foot seems tangled, but she is breathing," Billy commented about the woman. "Can you pull her free and see if she is ambulatory?" Jane asked.

Billy Dawes beckoned Silversmith to help him. Silversmith approached and tried to untangle the woman's ankle from the underbrush and surface roots, which appeared to have tripped her. Billy turned the woman over and dragged her to the road to lay the woman out flat.

Silversmith started to wipe away hair and blood from the woman's face with her hand to allow her to breath more easily.

"There is a pond two hundred yards yonder," Billy advised Silversmith, "Could you fetch some water?" Silversmith ripped a patch of torn cloth from the woman's skirts to act as a rag.

"Oh, the bottle in the carriage, could you fill that up, as well, Silversmith?" Jane asked.

Silversmith hurried off to the carriage to collect the empty bottle and then headed in the direction Billy indicated the pond was located.

"You were right to have stopped for this poor creature," Jane commended to Billy Dawes.

"She's been attacked, that's plain," Mr. Dawes explained, "It could happen to any one of us and we need to know we'll stop for one another to render aid."

Silversmith returned with a wet cloth to wipe the woman's face.

When the woman started to come to, Silversmith ran to the carriage to replace the now full water bottle and then returned to the side of the road with the others.

Jane spoke loudly bending over the woman on the ground. "Hello... Have you a name?" The woman jerked up, alert, uncertain where she was or who these people were.

"Oy." The woman said. "Where am I?"

Billy replied, "Along a road... betwixt civilized towns." The morning sun was just peeking out over the horizon.

"Have you a name, Miss?" Silversmith started, then seeing the woman's belly added, "Missus?" "Yes. Yes. Um," The woman said as she winced in pain, "Mulhoolin. Polly Mulhoolin."

"Oh, are you from Ireland?" Silversmith asked, "I'm a Contae Chorca lass."

"Down south? The old kingdom of Deas Mumhan? Founded as Cork in 1606? The home of the finest sailcloth?" Polly asked a bit surprised to have found somebody from her homeland.

"Aye," Silvesmith responded, "County Cork's Douglas sailcloth factory is the largest in all of Europe. The county also exports salted goods for long sea voyages. County Cork has also got O'Mahony's Woollen Mills in Blarney. Oh, and Sadleir's cotton mills in Glasheen, as well. Living near the ocean helped when my mistress, Miss Jane, and I sailed to these colonies," Silversmith shared with Polly.

"But doesn't Cork have English folk

living there?" Polly asked panicked.

"Cork 'twas also called Rebel City...it's heavily Protestant, you know..." Silversmith explained. "And your mistress... is she English?"

Silversmith seeing this woman agitated, calmly explained, "Polly, my father was a Johanna Meskill, my mother a Shiela. Both recruited by the group started in Limrick, the Buachaillí Bána, the blokes who wore white smocks."

"The Whiteboys, yes?" Polly said, "They defended the tenant farmer's land and fight against constant fees levied on the farmers and tithes the Anglican church demanded."

"They were called many names: Levellers, Queen Sive Oultagh's children, even fairies..." Silversmith sighed, "but although they wanted fairness, the fighting got my parent's killed. I was orphaned and the Hargreaves took me in as a servant. A salaried servant. Not a slave."

"So, your Mistress Hargreaves is English?" Polly asked cautiously.

"Yes...but she's not like the English you may be used to. She's a good soul, that is Miss Jane. My name is Silversmith? How shall I call you? Mrs. Mulhoolin?" Silversmith smiled realizing this Polly must be disoriented and weak.

"Nay. Polly," the weakened woman offered.

"By your accent," Silversmith observed, "I'd say you are from the north. County Ulster?"

"Yes. Originally, yes..." The woman replied, "It's nice to meet a sister from back home." Polly smiled as Billy Dawes carefully helped her to her feet.

Polly managed a curtsey.

"Oh, you are well brought up, then," Silversmith commented.

Silversmith turned to Jane and

whispered, "She's from your station, I'd say. She probably had tutors and such. Her clothes, tho, she probably had sewn them herself."

"Indeed?" Jane replied to Silversmith. To the woman, Polly, Jane said, "My name is Jane Hargreaves, this is my maid Silversmith and my driver, Mr. Dawes. Might I ask what befell you?"

"Oh, right," Polly started as she tried to stand without assistance, still very weak, "Um..." she shrugged.

"I see..." Jane replied and then whispered to Silversmith, "She's not very forthcoming with information. Do you think she is a criminal?"

"May I?" Silversmith asked Jane.

"By all means," Jane replied and stepped away a few feet to allow Silversmith to speak privately with this Polly woman.

Silversmith approached the woman

and lowered her voice. " Miss Hargreaves can be trusted. I'm not her slave, Polly. I stay in her employ of my own free will and she pays me regularly."

"But..." Polly hesitated.

"Polly, I can tell you are educated. I was not. I was an orphan. Miss Jane taught me to read and write. She sent me to school to learn of gardening and cooking. Her family never had slaves. They always paid their workers and each one was loyal to her because of the way she helped them be the best they could be within their station. I could easily find employment in any household I wish because of the education the Hargreaves gave me, but I choose to stay."

"I must be cautious," Polly emphasized.

"Miss Jane's got a good heart, that one. She was raised with one parent Jewish and one Christian. Miss Jane understands about how faiths conflict and she has a more forgiving heart because of it. She understands the Irish struggles with Catholics and Protestants. You realize, Polly, our carriage could have ridden on by, but we all stopped and are here to help you. Me, Billy Dawes, and especially Miss Jane. I don't see any other people around to help you," Silversmith reassured.

Nodding, Polly now approached Jane and shared, "Let me start anew, if I may. My name is Polly Mulhoolin. My husband and I built a cabin deep in the woods but it was attacked. They took or killed him and I escaped."

"You own land out here?" Jane clarified, wanting to, subtly, establish the class this Polly came from.

"My husband had paid the King's Lord Proprietor for all quit rent for the land, which has since been granted to us." Polly replied with an emotionless voice. "Part of the land is in the colony of Delaware... the headrighted acres lay in the colony of Maryland. We have not yet set up markers to identify our boundaries."

"Well, you must have given your attackers what for," Jane commented indicating the blood on Polly.

"Oh," Polly commented, now coming to grips with the fact that these people were here to help, not harm her, "Oh, this isn't my blood. It's from a pig. A wild boar."

"You provoked a wild beast?" Silversmith asked without thinking.

"No," Polly exclaimed, "I had succumbed to exhaustion, but stumbled upon a farrow of piglets and...well, I didn't want to, but had to defend myself."

"Come," Jane beckoned, "You must be weary from your ordeal." She guided the woman to the carriage. "Is there a friend in a nearby town we can take you to?" Jane offered.

"I am unfamiliar with these parts," Polly replied.

Jane turned to Billy Dawes, "Mr. Dawes," Jane started, "You've made deliveries off these roads."

"Yes, Miss Hargreaves," Billy Dawes replied.

"Is there an inn nearby where one might deposit this woman to be tended to?" Jane asked. Billy looked up and down the road, then took a deep breath before replying.

He said, "Mr. John Dunlap has a print shop in the next town. I've made several deliveries there. Not an inn, but they might have a spare room in their home. It won't be much out of our way. A quick stop to just outside of Philadelphia in the Pennsylvania Colony."

Silversmith asked Billy, "After we deliver Miss Polly to your Philadelphia friends, then can we continue on to Rising Sun in Maryland? Lady Sarah Wilson is expecting us at her estate."

"Oh, but I haven't money to pay for

lodgings. I haven't anything at all," Polly protested.

"I see," Jane paused as she calculated up the gold she had brought with her and the wisdom of bailing out every lost soul she may encounter along her voyage.

"Uh, Missus..." Billy Dawes drawled, "Where is the boar? The one you tangled with?"

"Um, Mulhoolin, uh, Gwinette..." Polly looked around confused to get her bearings, "I'm not sure where that sow..... Perhaps one or two hundred yards thence?" She pointed in the direction from which she came, "I think the pig is dead, but she is the size of a trunk." Polly indicated the large trunks strapped to the top of the carriage.

The sun languidly peered above the horizon, shedding morning light and long shadows on the party in the road.

"Well," Billy started, "Mr. Dunlap may appreciate a couple hundred pounds of fresh pork for his household."

"Oh, excellent thinking, Mr. Dawes," a delighted Jane replied. "Mr. Dawes, would you kindly fetch the pig to serve as payment for lodgings and then we can take this poor Miss... Miss..."

"Oh, please call me Polly," The woman shared with Jane. Then, to Billy Dawes, she added, "I think the creature was at least three hundred pounds."

Jane continued, "Even better. Yes, please fetch the pig for Polly's lodgings at this Dunlap residence you suggested."

"Aye," Billy replied, "It'll be a while, miss. I don't think I've the tools for butchering."

"Oh, I have," Silversmith offered.

"Silversmith," Jane explained, "You could help him."

Before Silversmith could answer, Billy added, "It won't be a pretty sight for a lady's maid to see."

Jane responded with, "She's not only my maid, she's everything else. Gardner, cook, seamstress inventor...she is amazing." She turned to Silversmith, "Yes, would you please help Mr. Dawes?"

"Yes, Miss Jane," Silversmith replied. Then, she turned to Billy, "I've packed my cooking knives up there. Can you fetch them for me?"

"Absolutely," Billy replied as he started to climb the mound of goods strapped to the carriage, looking for clues from Silversmith as to where they might be. "I'm a bit surprised you packed knives. Your butler told me you were heading to the opera..."

"Well, one never knows," Silversmith explained, "if our accommodation would require me to also cook, so I wanted to be prepared." Silversmith added, "I packed some sacs to contain Miss Jane's ...worn things... Perhaps?" She looked at Jane.

"Yes, yes," Jane replied, "By all means, use what you need to use."

"We can use the sacs to carry bits of the pig, once butchered," Silversmith explained to Billy Dawes, "They are over there..."

Once Billy found the needed tools, he jumped off the carriage. "It will take hours to boil all this up for stew... Perhaps some of it can be salted..."

"Oh, no," Silversmith explained, "The anglo Saxons would take the belly and fry it in a skillet. It's called bacoun and is actually crispy, not soft as when it's boiled. It is quick to make that way. I can show you which part of the belly to use."

"So we will present the Dunlaps with a house-guest and this bacoun as payment for her lodgings?" Billy Dawes clarified.

Silversmith replied, "When I was a girl, I was told a legend about a church in

Dunmow. Back in England it was. The church promised to give bacoun to any man who could swear before God that he had not argued with his wife for one year. If he had achieved this task, he could bring the bacoun home. The Church offered it as a prize. They even started a saying that a man who could bring home the bacoun was a man of grand character."

"Excellent ideas," Jane clasped her hands together."

She added, "If Silversmith can show the Dunlap cook different new ways to prepare this meat, then they will be more favorable to the idea of taking Polly in as a lodger until she is fit to travel again." Jane smiled at her maid, "Well done, Silversmith! Off you both go, then Polly and I will wait for you here at the carriage."

Jane turned to Polly. "Polly, do come and rest in the carriage. Let us see if we can clean off some of that dirt and blood before they return. We must present you properly to your new prospective landlords, the print-shop owning Dunlaps. We wouldn't want them to be frightened of you."

Polly looked at the carriage and into the forest, which soon swallowed up the departing Silversmith and Billy Dawes.

4 CHAPTER 22: (MARCH 1776) Button Runs

Ignoring the cracked leaves crunching beneath his feet, Button seized the moment.

He had just slipped out from under the blanket which pinned him in and now... while his captors still slept, he was going to run. He evaluated the costs of such a rash act and decided that If he simply stood there, they would kill him. If he remained, they might scalp him or sell him as a slave. Either way, his odds were better if he tried to run, so run he did.

Button ran throughout the night, distancing himself as much as he could, from the four mis-match Indian men who had held him captive for three days and nights. He needed to place as much distance between him and them as he could, lest they awaken and notice him missing.

Button zig-zagged his steps in an effort to avoid being tracked. He crossed puddles and small ponds, where he could. He assumed these men had the keen senses of a hunting dog.

After Button raced through a clearing, he came across a patch of trees, which were so dense the thick branches interlocked with the tree next to it.

Button decided to climb the first tree and travel from branch to branch toward the sound of water. Should they track him by footprints, he wanted to give them a new frustrating challenge.

Once in the tree branches, Button found the ability to maneuver from one to the next a great deal more challenging than he thought. Several times, he misjudged the sturdiness of the branch which should have held his weight and it started to crack. Once he saw a glimmer of the moon reflected in water, he landed on the ground and headed for the cool refreshing liquid.

Here he paused and drank, not realizing how thirsty he had become.

He reasoned the air was cool and the water even cooler, but he was quite warm indeed and didn't care about the shock of cold against his skin. He barely felt it, but knew he had to keep moving across to the opposite bank of this narrow brook.

Hoping it was not deceptively deep, he took a chance and splashed in up to his hips, wading across to the opposite bank. Then, despite the wet chafing trousers, he kept running. The trees were beginning to thin out and Button assumed this could be a sign of people having chopped down some trees to either make homes or clear a patch for grazing animals. Either way, he hoped it would be the right sort of people and did not wish to encounter another tribe.

Button had hoped to create such a complicated trail that the Indians would abandon the effort needed to chase him down.

Only adrenaline kept him going.

After, what he later estimated to be hours, he stopped to rest, but he found that he could not get up and instead he collapsed on the ground and got sick. He wiped his mouth and felt a headache coming on.

He glanced behind him and listened to see if he was being followed.

He looked up as he saw the moon was now fading into the dawn of morning. He crawled into a nearby two foot tall bush for camouflage. He waited.

Nobody came. Was it safe? Was he followed?

As the sun streaked across the sky, he noticed the bush where he had sought the shelter was a sweet pea plant, which had grown into a mound propped up by carefully placed sticks.

He picked one pea pod dangling right in front of him and ate it whole. He ate another and another. This was what his shaking body needed...nourishment.

He was laying face down in the dirt and when his hand grasped the earth, it was loose as if it had been plowed. He realized he must be on farmed land. Farmed land must mean a farmer is nearby and perhaps a village which could help him.

Now, with the light of early morning, Button could see over the horizon, peering out through the leaves of this vine.

He saw a figure moving with what appeared to be lumbering livestock. He couldn't tell if it was horses or oxen from this distance, but either way, he was pleased to see it.

He was about to cry out, but then thought if the Indians had been tracking him and were close, that would simply alert them and four expert hunters against two colonists was not good odds.

Instead, Button watched, exhausted, forcing his breath to be regular and steady. He popped his head up above the sweet-peas to get a better view of this farmer.

5 CHAPTER 23: (MARCH 1776) Polly and Jane Chat in the Carriage

Out on the road, Jane took a rather unlady-like step, hiked up her skirts and with Polly's help, entered the carriage. Polly came soon after, but with her wounded leg, it took Jane's tugging from inside to pull Polly up as well.

"Let's shut the door to keep all the animals out until Silversmith and Mr. Dawes return. It may be a while to butcher up that boar to serve as your pork payment for lodging, eh? But, that will give us time to clean you up a bit so we can meet the Dunlap family and convince them to take you in for a spell." Jane smiled as Polly closed the door behind her.

Jane reached under the carriage seat and produced a small carpet bag which, contained her hairbrush and other primping cosmetics.

"What is that?" Jane asked pointing to Polly's waist.

Polly, surprised, looked down at her waist to see a crumpled, bent bit rolled up paper in her apron string.

"Oh, I can't believe it is still there," Polly gasped as she pulled it out from her waistband. "What is it?" Jane asked.

"It is Vellum," Polly replied.

"Some sort of document?" Jane asked. Polly handed it to her and carefully, brushing away dirt, leaves and such,

Jane opened it, "It's blank," Jane commented.

"Yes," Polly said, "My husband was saving it for...something... I forgot it was still with me. I was going to put it someplace safe," Polly looked sad.

Jane took the crumpled paper and smiled, "We can get you a new one in town. Toss it away," Jane helpfully added.

"Oh, no." Polly withdrew the paper, "I must keep this one. I told him I'd put it someplace. It's from my husband."

Jane evaluated the distressed look of this woman clutching the blank sheet. "Silversmith is a marvel at these things. Place the object in my bag here, we'll keep it safe. Let's sort out your dress and get you situated. Perhaps the Dunlaps will have an idea about how to restore...not replace... this animal skin...or perhaps Silversmith can press this thing flat again... let's get to cleaning you up, shall we?"

Jane opened her carpet bag pointing to a side pocket inside. Polly deposited the paper into Jane's carpet bag hesitantly. Then, from within the bag, Jane withdrew a small bar of lavender soap and unwrapped the paper around it.

"What is Yardley?" Polly asked indicating the label. "Did you get that from a General Store?"

"No. Yardley is a small company from London. I brought this with me from home. Back a few years ago. Around 1770. William, or Mr. Yardley, used to sell swords and spurs and things to our friends. Then he started to sell soaps. "

"Why would a sword maker sell soaps?" Polly asked.

"Well, William Yardley's son-in-law, William Cleaver, had gambled away his inheritance. Mr. Yardley took over Mr. Cleaver's soap business to run it properly," Jane replied as she pulled at the jar of water.

Jane passed the bottle of water that Silversmith had filled from the pond earlier. She handed the soap, water and handkerchief to Polly. "I have faith in the management practices of Mr. Yardley. I was told that one day he plans on making colognes and lotions ..."

"It might be nice to have an unguent that does not come from the fat of animals...and, worse, smells like animals..." Polly reminisced as she unscrewed the small bottle of water, took her handkerchief, dipped it in gently, then rubbed the bar of soap onto the cloth before carefully returning it to the paper wrapper from which it had come.

Jane handed Polly the moist soapy handkerchief and another dry clean one. Polly accepted both, wiped her face with the damp cloth, then dried it with the other handkerchief.

Jane found a tiny pot of lip color and offered it to Polly with a gesture.

"Oh," Polly hesitated, "I thank you,

Miss Hargreaves, uh Jane... but I couldn't apply that to my lips. You see I am a married woman."

Jane paused a moment as she held the tiny pot of red lip color. She looked at this disheveled Polly and said, "Mrs. Mulhoolin, I..."

"Oh," Polly started, "MY name is Mulhoolin. My husband's name is Gwinette. Button Gwinette. Please call me Polly."

"You did not take your husband's surname?" Jane asked, surprised. "Polly...I'm Jane..." Jane smiled, then said, "Why don't we discuss the benefits and drawbacks of lip rouge in a moment. First, while I pull the twigs and dirt out of your hair with this ironically boar bristled brush, why don't you tell me all about how you met your husband, Mr. Button Gwinette."

"Have we the time?" Polly asked.

"Silversmith and Mr. Dawes will be a

while, yet butchering that wild pig. You know Silversmith knows so many novelties, such as this bacoun."

Jane smiled, "I'm sure she has to portion the boar in a certain manner, which will take even more time. Besides, won't it be fun to share your story? Then you would be my first British American sister I've befriended in this land."

Jane smiled urging Polly to share her story as Jane wondered what in her luggage she could lend to her new-found friend to make her more presentable to her future landlords. Besides, hearing Polly's story would be a welcomed distraction from Jane's recent unpleasantries.

6 CHAPTER 24: (MARCH 1776) The Farmer's Perspective.

With the cool morning sounds of birds awakening at the break of day, the farmer gazed along the horizon.

He needed the cart because he had to fill all those jugs in the back of the cart with water. After he delivered the water to town for that gentleman's meeting, he would return and harvest some of his sweet-peas for market.

The oxen trudged along, as he surveyed his crops. Then he saw something move. It wasn't the shape of wildlife he had become used to. He paused. He stopped the cart.

Was it an animal? The farmer yelled, "Hiaaaa," trying to shoo the beast, whatever it was away.

It didn't seem to scamper and run, as the farmer expected. Cautiously he approached. Stepping carefully between the plants to try and not crush too many of what could be picked and eaten, the Farmer approached the spot where he had seen the distraction.

When the farmer saw, what appeared to be a foot sticking out, the farmer asked, "Sir?" rather gruffly. Button moved slightly but found he could not speak, even though he wanted to.

"Sir?" the farmer asked again, this time kicking the foot. After all, it could be that this man was dead, could it not?

Button stirred and this frightened the farmer, who jumped back.

Button didn't realize how exhausted his limbs had become and was unable to move.

Cautiously, the farmer parted the vines of the sweetpeas covering Button and saw a man staring up at him, only able to blink.

The sturdy farmer looked back to his cart and then back at Button, then without a word, scooped up Button and carried him to his cart.

He had to move some jugs out of the way, but he found room for Button.

Button heard nobody else around and wondered if this Farmer lived alone.

"Sir?" The farmer asked again, but once more, Button was in no state to reply and could only blink.

Shrugging, the farmer poured some water from one of the nearly empty jugs onto Button's mouth.

This must have been the same sweet water as the water Button had just crossed to come to this farm.

It was especially good. The farmer reached into a basket and broke off a bit of cheese and put it in Button's mouth.

Button chewed. The farmer poured water on his lips again, then a bit of bread. Freshly baked but an hour before. The farmer had packed food to be out all day long.

Button closed his eyes and with the tiny bit of nourishment, he fell asleep.

The farmer shrugged to himself and guided the oxen onward to the stream ahead.

He did after all, have to fill all the jugs and make it to the gentleman's meeting.

Every gentleman's meeting was important and this farmer had a reputation of trust to maintain.

Finding this man in his patch of sweet peas mustn't delay him.

7 CHAPTER 25: (MARCH 1776) Button Awakens In Farmer's Cart

A bird shrieked, awakening Button, who sat up bolt upright in the back of a wooden cart. He looked around.

There was a man at the muddy bank of a broad brook, filling up empty jugs placed near the bank, and once full, he would place them in the cart, then return to the bank and fill up the next jug in line. The man at the bank was dressed in simple garb and appeared to be a farmer. Button was trying to gather his wits about him.

Where was he?

The sun was high. In front of him was the water. He looked behind him and saw the cart was tethered to oxen, who were grazing on the tall grasses at their feet.

Button didn't realize he had succumbed to slumber and now was...was...where was Button? "Pardon me, do you speak English?" Button asked.

The man, presumably a farmer, stood up and walked over to Button.

"Yes," The man replied. He reached across to grab a basket. Once he pulled the basket closer to him, he withdrew a hunk of cheese and handed it to Button along with a jug he had just filled up.

"Thank you, thank you so much," said Button as he accepted the cheese and water. A moment later, he felt much better. Not ready to charge into battle, but not about to faint, either.

"I have," Button didn't quite know how to phrase his sentence, "I have escaped from scalpers."

The farmer nodded, then turned away to fill up the rest of the empty jugs he had laid in a row by the brook bank.

Button eased out of the cart asking, "May I help you? I'm most appreciative of the food and if this is your task, I would like to assist, if I may?"

The farmer paused, looked at Button, then handed him an empty jug.

Button filled it up, as he had seen this farmer do it. Then he walked to the cart and placed the full jug in the cart.

Attempting to start a conversation, Button shared, "I came to these lands four or five years ago. I'm sure each person here has left something behind for the hope of a better future. When did you get here?"

The farmer handed Button another empty jug.

"The first step," Button started, "is getting here. The second step is figuring out what skill you can exchange for bread. The third step is negotiating all the campaigns of different countries vying to own different parts of this land, eh?"

"Power," the farmer replied. "Those that have, may compromise values to keep power."

"Oh! You do speak English! Splendid!" Button was relieved.

He didn't want to encounter another few days of speaking to somebody who couldn't communicate with him.

"Right you are. What is the cost of this

concept called freedom?" Button added, "My name is Gwinette. Button Gwinette," Button shared smiling, with arm outstretched to shake hands, as gentlemen do.

The farmer simply continued to fill the jugs. Button took his outstretched arm and directed it to an empty five gallon jug, then stepped to the bank, filling it with water and bringing it to the cart.

The farmer also filled his five gallon jug and walked to the cart saying, "Another pioneer. Another settler. Another soul in trouble."

"Pardon me?" Button asked.

"You," The less than verbose farmer exclaimed, "are indeed a troubled soul."

"Right," Button said to himself, "the pleasure is all mine..." He trailed off. Then more clearly asked, "What are all these water jugs for?"

The farmer explained, "Meeting in town."

"Ah," Button stood with his hands on his hips looking at the multiple jugs, "But don't most towns possess wells? Or their own source of water?"

"Mine tastes better," The farmer replied, "for a private meeting."

"Ah, a particularly discriminating clientele. I understand," Button sympathized, "Might I come to town with you? Don't want to tempt those wilderness-loving scalpers, you see. Would welcome some civilization."

"I see," the farmer replied.

Only the sounds of wildlife, babbling water tumbling over smooth stones and boulders, and the occasional snort of the oxen surrounded the men as they deftly filled the jugs with water.

Button heard a twig snap in the distance away from where the oxen stood. Suddenly alert, Button wondered if he was being watched by his captors. Was he too sloppy in trying to hide his tracks? Would this farmer be a worthy comrade in battle?

Button asked again, "Could I help you with getting to your meeting?"

"It's tomorrow," The Farmer clarified, "more over the next couple of months or so..."

Button smiled politely trying not to alarm the farmer, "We seem awfully..." Button struggled for the correct words to speak through a smile, "...exposed in your beautiful land, here. I would think your discriminating clientele would like their sweet water delivery promptly..."

"... I would very much like to help you make your customers happy by delivering it early."

"You'll help serve at the meetings?"

"Yes. Indeed," Button emphatically

agreed, "all the meetings for the next couple months. Sounds lovely. I can't wait."

"You a gentleman, Sir?"

"Uh. Well, I was raised to be an educated man back in England, but I do or did work. My wife and I are trying to live independ...were... we... she... were... Why do you ask?"

"You said," the farmer replied, "You'd help. Wondered if you meant it."

Button saw a lower tree branch wavering and he couldn't be sure if it was caused by an animal or one of his captors aiming an arrow at him.

"Yes, yes... shall we go?" Button started taking all the jugs, empty or not, and loading them onto the cart.

"A gentleman's word is like a contract," The farmer explained. "Yes, yes, Yes," Button hurried.

The farmer placed stoppers on all the open jugs in the cart, then sat on the bench of the cart and started to urge the oxen forward, as if they were horses.

"Will you keep it?" the farmer asked.

"Keep what?" Button inquired keeping pace along side the slow moving cart. "Words," the farmer responded.

"Yes. I've noticed in these parts there seems to be quite an aversion to words. Not many words bandied about by those who live in these lands, are there?" Button smiled.

"Keep," the farmer emphasized.

"Words? Yes," Button replied with a pious expression, "Every last word. All of them. Now, shall we be off to town?"

Button looked to the farmer awaiting permission to climb up alongside the farmer in the slow moving cart.

The farmer patted the empty spot where he had reclined earlier. Button hopped into the back of the cart, taking that to be an invitation as he nestled himself among the water jugs.

Button saw a concerned expression on the farmer's face.

It appeared as if the farmer was deciding if Button would honor his agreement or if he was merely being flippant.

Button was eager to establish an alliance and make a new friend, as much as he wanted to get to a town. Once in a town, he could seek assistance with getting home.

He could find out if other colonists were being captured by Indians in the vicinity, as he had been.

Most of all, he wanted to find out if there was a chance his wife was still alive.

If she did survive, she would have made it to a town and the gossip between towns would spread her story. He could inquire at the local coffee house, if there was one, or wherever the news is shared.

If he could inquire about a pregnant woman who escaped an attack, then he could probably find where she was lodging and make his way to her.

The fact that Button was viewed with suspicion by the farmer, did not surprise him. His clothes were tattered and although his speech betrayed an education, his appearance did not. There were several charlatans travelling these parts, ready to take advantage of a gullible victim. Perhaps this farmer was wondering if Button was one of those vipers.

He wondered had he found a ragged man on his own lands, would he react the same way? He may be even more harsh than this farmer was to him. Button might even demand a stranger leave immediately instead of feeding him cheese and fresh water from the stream, as this farmer had kindly done.

It was important to Button to prove he was trustworthy to this farmer... It did not matter which town he went to, he simply needed to get to any form of civilization and safety.

Serving water for a few weeks was worth the price. Plus, this farmer would likely have enough food to feed Button while he was helping with this water thing. Button knew he did not have money to buy food, so he had to use what he did have. Right now, he had his ready-to-help hands.

Button needed time to recuperate and determine what to do next.

"Yes," Button smiled as he moved around, careful not to tip over any of the filled water jugs in the cart as the oxen lumbered along, pulling the cart away from the exposed bank.

Button continued, "I am a gentleman and I will help you serve water at whatever meetings you require. My word, sir. I will keep my word to you."

8 CHAPTER 26: (1770-six years ago) Polly Meets Button at the Docks

Polly thought back six years and shared her story with her new friend Jane Hargreaves, who was now helping her clean up before taking her to the Dunlaps as a potential lodger.

It was 1770, Polly recalled, and the salty air of the docs smelled odd to Polly, who had arrived from the lush grassy lands of Ireland.

<><><>

Polly had signed her contract.

As was customary with contracts of indentured servitude, the man used a blade to cut the parchment upon which the contract was written. The cut was zig zagged neatly across the parchment, and he gave half to Polly.

"The other half of this contract will be delivered to your master in the Americas," the man explained, then added, "You best be getting to that big ship."

Polly looked behind her. There was a line of other Irish men and women who had already endured a stressful journey from their native Ireland to England, and now they were to set sail to the British colonies across the vast ocean.

"You are certain the term is for four years…not seven," Polly wanted to verify the duration of her indentured servitude.

"Four years," the man said to Polly Mulhoolin, and then shouted to the girl standing behind her, "Next!" Before Polly left she said, "Please, sir, Please write four years on my half as well. I'll wait."

Annoyed, the man took the two pages, placed them together. He found the sentence which stated that in exchange for Polly Mulhoolin's passage to the British American colonies, she would be a house servant to a family until 1774. After which, she would then have fulfilled her contract and be considered a free woman once more.

Four years...not seven.

"Thank you, Mr. Broker, sir," Polly said as she took her half and placed it carefully in her bodice next to her heart.

Nothing was going to happen to that bit of paper.

When Polly got to the docks, she saw various passengers gathered to board ships. Some appeared well to do.

She used to be 'well to do...' before her village was raided and all the men, including her father, were taken by the British Crown. Apparently, being Catholic irritated the British and the choice was to either die in prison or become a slave.

Her father and other able-bodied men of the village were taken by force, shipped to one of the tropical British colonies, deprived of all human dignity, to serve as slaves.

Her mother had discussed options and they knew it was a matter of time before another raid would take the women and children next.

Her mother had urged her to go to England, find a broker, and accept a position as an indentured servant in exchange for passage to the British Americas. She'd get room and board and avoid slavery.

"It will be a sacrifice, but you'll be free once again, and you can make a better life in a new land where the King doesn't have as much influence," her mother advised her. "I'm too old to be a servant, but not too old to be taken as a slave, so I will try to find a position in a church and if God wills it, I'll head for the Americas, as well."

Her mother started to recite, "Why have I a heart so constant? Cruel love! O Waly, Waly up the bank. Farewell, farewell, all hope of bliss! For Polly always must be thine. Shall she my heart be never his, which never can again be mine?"

"Mother," Polly asked, "Why do you quote The Beggar's Opera?"

Her mother continued, "Because your father took me to that opera. Twice. We had so much fun, then..."

"...and that song reminds me of your father...and it will remind me of you...once I let you go." "Mama?" Polly asked, confused,

"You must go to a new life in the Colonies..." Her mother looked down and continued to hum, "Oh love you play a cruel part...."

Polly completed the tune, "...you should reward a constant heart since alas 'tis so seldom found..."

"You skipped a bit, there, Polly," Her mother smiled, "I know the Polly in that story is not you, but that part from now on... It will always remind me of you..."

"Mama," Polly had said, "You are not Catholic. Being Protestant should protect you."

"A stóirín..." Her mother started to say, "Oh, my little dear...I'm a Protestant, but married to a Catholic. These men come for slaves. Cheap labor. After a while they won't stop at Catholic men, they will take in other races, other religions... it is all about getting cheap labor so merchants can make an even... bigger" "profit..."

"But they say it is because of Catholic..." Polly protested.

Her mother corrected her, "Remember that if you witness an atrocity visited upon a neighbor, it is but a matter of time before the same act will happen to you...unless you do something about it."

"But I don't want to leave..." Polly protested.

"You must leave. On your own. The journey will be hard, but ...." Her mother encouraged. "But don't you think you'll see Papa again?" Polly asked.

"Polly. Your father was killed. We must accept that and make choices to protect ourselves."

"No. No, that cannot be..."

"Polly, listen to me." Her mother took her sternly by the shoulders. "It is better for you to leave now and take a servant position. Please. If you wait... If you do nothing... Some entitled fool will rip your freedom from you and you will never experience freedom again. Now go. Work with diligence. Do not focus on the atrocities you might witness...Nay, you will witness them. Keep to yourself when you are a servant..."

"...When your contract is fulfilled, you shall live... your... life..."

With that, Polly had packed an abundance of food for her journey and remembered her mother's words. The mother she would never see again.

9 CHAPTER 27: (1770) Polly At The Docks

As Jane Hargreaves combed out the brambles and leaves from Polly's hair to make her presentable to the Dunlaps, Polly continued with her tale.

It was a long wait in the crowd before boarding commenced. Polly had to sleep on her food hamper to protect its contents. She was uncertain she would get food and water aboard the ship and she had to prepare for the long journey across the Western ocean.

Before Polly's father was taken away, he had one of the staff put wheels on a hamper. Polly used this to store her food for the voyage. She had, as well, wool clothing to combat the elements. She had left all her finery at home.

It would do her no good in her new role as indentured servant.

At the docks, Polly kept silent so the British in the crowd might not detect her Irish brogue. Many were engaged in conversation, but Polly could not help overhear the couple closest to her.

The man seemed distressed because the lady was pressing him to accept what appeared to be a list on rather fine parchment.

"This list!" the man started, "They will

not permit me to take all this luggage aboard, my love," the man said to his lady friend while looking at the parchment.

"Your plans to marry in those colonies once we arrive are absurd," the woman retorted, "How am I to survive over there without the proper wardrobe? Reginald would never do this."

"Why do you bring up Reginald, again, my love. You said you wanted to get married. I told you the company I work for is asking me to go to the Americas to some colony called Georgia and that is where we shall marry. If you like we can ask the captain of this vessel to marry us at once," the man tried to reason.

Polly witnessed a small boy creep up behind the man.

The boy carefully extracted a small red and blue velvet pouch out of the man's jacket pocket. Polly reasoned this was the man's coin purse.

Then, the woman turned around as another man, dressed in a sharp official uniform came running toward her, gathering her into his arms.

"My darling!" this second man cried, "Do not abandon me to that uncivilized island. Stay with me, I beg you."

Meanwhile, the boy had taken the pouch and casually slipped it under his tattered hat.

"Uh, Pardon me, Reginald," The first man cleared his throat, "But we are about to walk aboard..."

"Oh, Reginald," the woman sighed, grasping this man in relief, "I didn't think you felt that way about me..."

The second officially dressed man clasped the woman to his chest with a firm embrace sighing as he rested his chin atop her head, but then gingerly moved his chin as he became aware that she had some decorative hair accents which were becoming dislodged as a result of his grasp.

Then the boy who took the velvet pouch started walking casually toward Polly.

Quickly, Polly grasped the boy by his collar and whisked off his hat, with the pouch of money still inside it.

"Oi!" The boy cried, "let me be," he shouted at Polly and then noticing his hat was gone yelled, "you stole from me. Give it back."

His cries drew the attention of the two men and one woman standing nearby.

The man called Reginald looked away and gazed into the eyes of the woman he was holding. The other man saw the boy and felt in his pocket and noticed his purse was gone.

This other man started toward Polly who was still holding the boy. "If," Polly said, "I took something from you, tell me what it is." The boy replied, "It's money.

You took my money."

The man had now approached Polly, but did not yet speak.

"And what color is this money pouch?" Polly demanded of the boy. "Color? Black? Uh... Brown... It's mine. Give it back." The boy cried. Polly released the boy, clapped the hat smartly back on the boy's head.

She then turned to the man now standing next to her and said, "I saw this lad take your blue and red velvet bag. Allow me to return it to you, the rightful owner." She turned to the boy and said, "You have a choice, you know. You should choose to do what is right next time... now be off with you."

"You are Irish." The man replied, "and you saw him steal from me and you stopped it?"

"Aye," Polly replied, "I've got a problem with your king and politics, not with the people. When something is wrong, it should be righted. That's what my mama would say. I think I taught him a lesson and next time he thinks about stealing, he should think twice..."

"Really," Button seemed impressed with Polly's integrity, "I didn't realize the Irish invented right and wrong." He smiled.

"Of course we did. We invent lots of things, you know." Polly smiled back playfully. "As in..." Button prompted.

"How about a pint of Guinness from Leixlip in County Kildare. Did you know that Arthur Guinness so believed in his beer that in 1759 he signed a 9,000 year lease at St. James' Gate Brewery?"

"I did not know that," he laughed, "My name is Button Gwinette. Are you from County Kildare in Ireland?"

"I'm from County Ulster," Polly grinned, "A free educated lass who is now seeking passage to the Colonies as *Endenteure*..."

"Ah, yes." Button reasoned, "The indentation to take a parchment contract and cut it on a crooked line to show ownership for a specific time period. Once your half fits your employer's half then you can prove the contract terms are valid and you are free..."

Polly muttered, "I am certain the old French word is used because the beautiful English language does not have a single word to denote a contract between a master and mutually agreed upon services rendered by an apprentice, such as myself."

A few feet away the woman who was standing next to this Reginald fellow exclaimed, "Button! Is that your mistress?"

The man said to Polly, "Thank you very much for retrieving my stolen money pouch."

The man Polly now knew as Button, then turned to his lady friend and said, "She was doing me a kindness, my love."

The woman retorted, "If you treat me this way before our voyage, I will not go on that voyage!" The woman emphatically folded her arms, turning toward Reginald.

Button looked at Polly helplessly. Reginald stood there with a scowl on his face as he reached out to the wounded lady friend. She then promptly sat down defiantly on a pile of steamer trunks and clothing caskets.

Polly said, "That ramp... I'm going up that ramp to board the ship, Mr. Gwinette, I'll leave you to it." She headed up the ramp and was very tempted to look back to see what would happen next.

10 CHAPTER 28: (1700) Polly on the Ship

Jane Hargreaves leaned back in the carriage and asked Polly Mulhoolin, "Then what happened when you were aboard the ship?"

<><><>

After three days on the ship, Polly ran into Button Gwinette.

He disclosed to Polly that his lady friend had decided to stay with Reginald, after all. He thanked Polly for her kindness as that pouch contained all the money he had. He realized she could have even taken it for herself, but chose not to.

She chose to do what was right.

"This voyage will last almost two months, Miss Mulhoolin. If you don't mind, I would very much enjoy your companionship, at your convenience," Button Gwinette shared.

Polly agreed.

Button had a cabin.

Polly found quickly she was neither permitted to make her way to the upper decks, nor to descend to the lower ones. Button, on the other hand, was free to venture from his upper deck to the lower decks.

With waves continually rocking the

boat, Polly vowed that she would live as far inland as she could get in order to be away from the ocean. She had already become sick on the voyage, finding it rather miserable except for her new friendship with Button.

Button entertained her, when he visited her on the middle deck. He was always respectful, never insinuating that she should be anything more than a friend.

The ship was divided into three groups: Upper decks for the paying passengers who could afford cabins, such as Button Gwinette.

Indentured Servants, such as Polly, were in the middle decks. These passengers were promised to a colonist and were being delivered like cargo.

The lower decks were for the third group. Every inch of the floor was covered with these people sleeping head to toe. They were meant to be slaves. Their lot was the worst.

They had to sleep in their own filth battling hunger, fear and the stench of their own sicknesses, including fever, seasickness, boils, and mouth rot.

The food they had was dried salted meats and some grains. These caused thirst, but the water to drink was foul.

The slaves were considered disposable.

Polly saw some of these being tossed overboard during the voyage. She prayed these souls were already dead before being dispatch thusly. There was one incident, which she would never forget. The one that happened to her.

After a gale wind rocked the boat for nearly two full days, Polly overheard one of the crew saying, "We are short on supplies. We don't have food to last for three more weeks."

"What are we to do?" the other crewman asked.

There was a pause, then the captain

said, "Take the sick and the slaves, especially the sickly Irish, and toss them overboard. Then there should be enough food to last us all."

Polly didn't think she heard correctly. It was at this time, she was happy she learned to speak German and French fluently as she decided to speak in that language.

One by one, she witnessed men and women mercilessly being tossed overboard.

And, for a while, she thought she was safe. Her ruse of speaking in a foreign tongue had worked... until one crew member grabbed Polly by the wrist.

"Oi." he said, "this one's got extra food in this hamper." He flung open the hamper to reveal her dried oats and fruits she was nibbling on to keep her alive, "We can toss 'er over..." and he shoved Polly to another crew mate as he delved into Polly's hamper of food.

As Polly was being dragged to the railing of the boat, she heard a familiar voice shout at the man. "Stand down, Sir." Button cried, "That is my property you have there!"

"What?" The deckhand turned around to face Button with Polly still in his grasp, "The indentured servants are meeting their owners when we dock. She ain't yours!"

Button strode confidently toward the gruff sailor holding Polly, as he shoved a crumpled paper into Polly's hand. With a flourish, Button produced another half parchment and said, "These are my papers. Ask her if she has the other half to prove I'm the owner."

The crewman looked at Polly and said, "Well? 'Ave you got it?"

Without a word, Polly handed the crewman the paper Button had just shoved in her hand.

The crewman fit the two pieces

together and with a sneer he said to his fellow crew member, "Get out of her hamper of food! This gentleman owns her. It's his property!" The crewman shoved the papers back at Button and then shoved Polly into Button's arms as he went off to look for another passenger to throw overboard.

"Steady there, Miss Mulhoolin," Button whispered.

Polly looked at the papers the crewman had returned to Button. She looked at them closely.

"These," Polly whispered as she quietly looked up from the papers into Button's eyes, "this is a list of finery for a lady's wardrobe."

"Yes," Button admitted. "My lady friend, the one who stayed behind, felt one must always use the finest paper for everything, even a list you intend to toss away. She feels it will impress others. The parchment, however, is of the quality of contracts, so I took a chance..."

"But..." Polly stuttered, still shaken.

"I took a chance that a sailor can read the stars, but not words on a page. He just needed to see the two halves fit and that I was here to claim my property," Button explained.

"Oh, my mother...my mother would have said that I hid and I did nothing to help the others," Polly's heart sank.

"You cannot," Button explained, "Blame yourself for how these sailors view the Irish or the other slaves," Button consoled. Your first order of business is to stay alive, get prepared, then you can make a concerted difference. "

"As a slave?" Polly softly asked, bewildered. "Did you know that the first Irish slave was sold over a century ago in 1612 to a settlement along the Amazon River? My people are always going to be a pool of cheap labor."

"You are not a slave, you are indentured and you will be free one day," Button reminded her. "In a new land. With new rules."

"I'm going to miss you when I start my term in my master's household," Polly whispered, "You saved my life just now."

"Well, you'll be living at one address, which is penned on your half of your contract. So, give me that address and I will write to you. That way we can continue our friendship, if that is agreeable to you, Miss Mulhoolin."

"Oh, do call me Polly. I would be very happy to correspond with you."

11 CHAPTER 29: (1770-1774) After Polly Landed in the Colonies

Jane, wide-eyed, closed the carpet bag next to her on the carriage bench seat. She asked Polly, "Once Button rescued you from that sailor who had endeavored to throw you overboard, pray, tell me what happened."

Polly continued her story.

Button made it a practice to visit Polly at every opportunity in the middle decks to verify she was still safe.

When the ship finally docked at the Colonial port in the New world, Polly found the family she was to work for.

The family was pleased to see her because it meant with her arrival, the family was also granted one headright which meant they could now claim an additional fifty acres of land to increase their estate.

Polly did not tell them that she was looking at the next few years as a way to learn how to cultivate the soil so that once she was free, she could do the same with her own plots of land. Polly was educated enough to read up on how things worked. Most women in her situation did not know how to read, so this gave Polly an advantage.

The family had both slaves and servants. Polly, as a servant with a clear end date to her contract, she counted herself lucky.

As an unmarried Irish woman, during her tenure, she was not forced to marry anybody to breed more slaves. She reminded the family that they can easily increase their acreage if they sponsored a new servant to be shipped over instead of simply breeding them.

Polly quickly found herself busy minding the master's children. She determined to never complain of hard labor. Once, Polly mentioned to the lady of the house that if she, an indentured servant, were ever to have children of her own, it would deplete her time and energies to properly care for the master's dear children.

Because Polly was educated, she was not only a housemaid, but also a tutor to the children. This presented its own challenges when they misbehaved.

In other households, Polly found that the Irish slaves were valued at one tenth the price of imported African slaves.

Some entrepreneurial small businesses knew this and started to force young Irish slave girls to mate with black slave men to create a bargain black slave since the Irish were the lowest valued.

Polly read in an act concerning slaves in the Maryland Assembly Proceedings of September 1664, that if the father was enslaved, any children would also belong to the master of the father because serving Durante Vita, meant they were enslaved for the duration of their lives.

Back around 1681, this practice became outlawed because it cut into the profits of those more prosperous slave traders who had genuine black slaves for sale, not the cheap Irish imitation black slaves. The legislation stated, "...forbidding the practice of mating Irish slave women to African slave men for the purpose of producing slaves for sale."

The Company of Royal Adventurers Trading to Africa, founded in 1660, had run into trouble with the war with Holland in 1667, but in 1672 it was reformed as The Royal African Company, which procured a monopoly on the African and Irish slave trade, transporting about 5,000 per year on 249 shiploads from Africa to the Indies and British American Colonies.

About 23% of their cargo died during transport.

In 1698, English Parliament saw how lucrative it was and opened the slave trade to all willing businesses, which meant English ships now transported four times the yearly amount, or 20,000 persons a year...including the Irish. Then, a new small business was born: The make your own imitation African slaves here...they were the mixed race.

The law said that if a male slave had a child, that child would also be a slave and serve "Durante Vita" or hard labor for life. If the child was of mixed heritage, the child would serve until 21 years of age. So, these businesses decided to breed mixed races with the father being of African descent. Even if the father was "free", just having a mixed child would force the father to serve a master for at least 7 years...or longer.

This *Durante Vita* law applied to black male slaves and white women marriages. It also noted how some masters connived to exploit the law by forcing freeborn female indentured Irish servants to "marry" for the purposes of having children born into slavery for the master's use as that child would be a slave for 21 years[1].

Polly once saw a copy of the Maryland Acts of the General Assembly, April 1684-June 1692 and noted that a master who wanted to extend a contract beyond 7 years, could compel a mixed couple to have a child.

That would provide the master with a free slave for 21 years and both parents would need to recommit to an additional 7 years each of servitude, even if one of the parents was already free.

---

[1] Archives of Maryland, ed. William Hand Browne et al. (in progress; Baltimore, 1883 to date), Assembly Proceedings, May 10-June 9, 1692 Vol 13, P. 547

Polly thought... 1681...It was the same year the colony of Maryland reversed an earlier law. That Colony allowed both children born to free black women and black children born to white women to truly be born free. Being a mixed breed of white and black...or a "mule", as they were called, these children were sometimes referred to as a Mulatto man or Mulatta woman. These offspring were branded, like any commercial product, as a home-grown imitation African slave, a bargain. The mixed children were not one of those expensive slaves directly shipped over from Africa.

It was not a crime, Polly found, to kill an Irish slave.

It was considered a financial setback for the owner who found it cheaper to kill a slave from Ireland, than to harm a slave from Africa.

To deliberately kill a disobedient Irish slave was a financial inconvenience for the master. To maim or kill a pure bred African slave, which was valued at ten times the Irish equivalent, was a major financial loss.

Luckily, Polly was a servant not a slave and she had a date when she would be set free. 1774. She was very mindful to obey every order to the letter because the punishment for not obeying was abundantly harsh, sometimes involving fires or beating to death.

Polly was educated and knew her history.

She had cursed dead King James the VI of Scotland who had started this madness against the Irish by selling 30,000[2] of them into slavery in the early 1600's. Over half of the inhabitants of Antigua and Montserrat were Irish slaves[3]. Later, the West Indies and

---

[2] In April 1653, Cromwell's Council of State issued licenses for Sir John Clotworthy to transport five hundred Irishmen to America, with eight thousand more in June 1653. He later received a license to transport four hundred Irish children to New England and Virginia (Jordan & Walsh, 2008)

[3] Peter Williamson chronicled in his memoir of his abduction from his homeland in Ireland in 1743 at the age of thirteen and is recorded in Jordan & Walsh, 2008, p.237-239...

Jamaica and even the colonies of Virginia and New England, were flooded with Irish slaves and servants.

Polly realized that all the colonies had Irish to do the hard labor along side the genuine imported-from- Africa- slaves.

King James the VI's son, Charles, believed God gave him the right to behave any way he wished even if the law forbade it.

He made himself king over Ireland, and made the entire country a pool of cheap human livestock for the merchant classes to exploit. The Calvinists, the Puritans and Protestants all disagreed with him.

One hundred years later, now that King George William Fredrick sat on the English throne, the resentment of the Irish was still fresh. This king also lusted after the mysteries of the African continent and was engaged in several wars.

In spite of all the horrors, Polly desperately focused on the positive as she continued to correspond with Button.

They discussed it in a letter. If they married, it would be best to do it in secret. For him to marry an Irish woman publicly would hurt his business reputation.

Polly agreed. Some things have to remain secret.

The year and day her contract came due, her master tried to tell her that her contract was for seven, not four years.

Polly retrieved her half of the contract and aligned the two parts of the parchment along the zig zag. Clearly, the terms read four years, not seven and she was now eligible to be a free woman as of 1774.

It took some convincing with the help of Button Gwinette, but she was ultimately released as a free woman.

Soon thereafter, Button Gwinette and Polly Mulhoolin married, but kept their separate surnames.

"One day," Button promised, "it will be safe to change your name, but for now...I'd rather keep you alive."

"It is only a matter of time," Polly whispered on their secret wedding day, "That the Irish will rise up against the British, but I want you to know I will always be on your side because I know you are there for me."

For now, Polly could live with Button in a remote place.

"Button, What do you think," She asked searching for the right words, "about...Well...Perhaps we could live in the woods... away from the ocean..."

Button added, "And where nobody would bother us. Where we could build a family in peace..."

12 What Just Happened?

As Polly pushes herself to survive, and tries to also grasp onto the hope that Button is still alive somehow, Jane, her new friend, has put aside her own struggles for justice to help out somebody less fortunate.

Meanwhile, we learn of Polly's perilous journey to the Colonies and how she first met Button back in the 1770's.

13 Did You Know...

INDENTURED

Leaving your home country is difficult, In this story, Polly sold herself as an indentured servant for a number of years just to pay for her passage to an unknown land for an unknown future. This was a way many people chose to get themselves to America. Indentured servitude was voluntarily contracted for a specified limited time, and was not considered slavery.

Colony of Maryland Slave Codes

An Act Concerning Negroes & Other Slaves

Assembly Proceedings, September 1664

An Act Concerning Negroes & other Slaues

Bee itt Enacted by the Right Honble the Lord Proprietary by the aduice and Consent of the upper and lower house of this present Generall Assembly That all Negroes or other slaues p. 29 already within the Prouince And all Negroes and other slaues to bee hereafter imported into the Prouince shall serue Durante Vita And all Children born of any Negro or other slaue shall be Slaues as their ffathers were for the terme of their liues And forasmuch as divers freeborne English women forgettfull of their free Condicōn and to the disgrace of our Nation doe intermarry with Negro Slaues by which alsoe diuers suites may arise touching the Issue of such woemen and a great damage doth befall the Masters of such Negros for preuention whereof for deterring such freeborne women from such shamefull Matches Bee itt further Enacted by the Authority advice and Consent aforesaid That whatsoever free borne woman shall inter marry with any slaue from and after the Last day of this present Assembly shall Serue the master of such slaue dureing the life of her husband And that all the Issue of such freeborne woemen soe marryed shall be Slaues as their fathers were And Bee itt further Enacted that all the Issues of English or other freeborne woemen that haue already marryed Negroes shall serve the Masters of their Parents till they be Thirty yeares of age and noe longer.

Children Born to Slaves: 1600's

The Maryland Assembly Proceedings, May 10 to June 9, 1692. had strict rules regarding slavery. A child born to a mixed-race couple would mean that child was a slave until the age of 21. An "English born" woman who had a mixed child would need to serve for 7 years. If she was already a servant, she needed to finish her first 7 years, then serve an additional 7 years for a total of 14 years of service.

The same rules applied if a white male servant had a child with a woman of another race. If one parent was "free", then they gave up their freedom for 7 years. The slave master owned everything. Some slaves served for life. Other "indentured servants" had a term of 7 years. If a legal marriage took place between a mixed heritage couple, then the priest would be fined 10 thousand pounds of tobacco and the master would relinquish ownership and also pay the king 10 thousand pounds of tobacco.

Here are some **excerpts** of the original text of Maryland Assembly Proceedings,in the **original language as written in the 1600s**.

An Act concerning Negro Slaves.

Be it Enacted by the King and Queens most Excellent Majesties by and with the Advice and consent of this prsent Generall Assembly and the Authority of the same, That all negroes and other slaves already imported or hereafter to be Imported into this Province, shall serve their naturall lives and all the Children born already or hereafter to be born of any Negroes or other Slaves withn this Province shall be Slaves to all intents and purposes as their parents were for the terme of their naturall lives And forasmuch as diverse free born English and white women, sometimes by the Instigation procurement or Conivance of their Masters Mistress or Dames,...

Satisfaction of their Lacivious lustfull desires,... .do somtimes intermarry with and Sometimes permitt themselves to be gotten with child by negros or other Slaves...the issue of Children of such English or White women as aforesaid,...

That any freeborn English or white woman that shall after the Publication of this Law, either intermarry with or permitt herself to be begotten with child by any Negro or other Slave, shall undergo the paines and penalties by this Law hereafter provided against them, That is to say any free born English or white woman be shee free or Servant and shall hereafter intermarry with any negro or other Slave or to any Negro made free, shall Imediatly upon such Marriage forfeit her freedome and become a Servant during the Terme of seven years....

if he be a free Negro or Slave to whom she intermarried, he shall thereby also forfeit his freedome and become a Servant...during his naturall life...she shall become a Servant during the Terme of Seven years...

till they arive to the Age of one and twenty years... And if any free woman or Servant as aforesaid shall permitt themselvs to be begotten with child by any Negro or Slave not marryed together as aforesaid, shall for every such Offence suffer the pains and penalties hereafter menconed ...

If a free woman at the time of the begetting or bearing of such Bastard Child as aforesaid, she shall become a Servant and Serve to the uses aforesaid during the space of seven years to commence from the time of her delivery of such bastard Child as aforesaid, and if he be a free Negro or Slave...

the said free Negro shall likewise become a

Servant for seven years to the use aforesaid to comence from the time of the womans delivery as aforesaid But if the woman be a Servant at the time of such begetting and bearing of such Bastard Child as aforesaid she shall first serve out her first time of Servitude ...

and after shall serve the Term of Seaven years as aforesaid to commence from the finishing her first Service as aforesaid...and all such Bastard Children to be Servants to the uses aforesaid till they arrive to the age of thirty one years ...

And be it Enacted by the Authority aforesd by and with the consent and advice aforesaid that any freeborn English or white man that shall from and after the Publication of this Act eitherinter marry wth or begett with Child any negro woman or Slave when proved against him shall be lyable to the same paines and penalties as in and by this Act is provided against English or white woman...

...That if any Master Mis-tress or dame having any free born English or white woman Servant as aforesaid in their Possession or propriaty shall by any Instigation procurement, knowledge permission or Conive-ance whatsoever suffer any such freeborn English or white woman Servant in their Possession & wherein they have pro-priety as aforesaid to

Intermarry or contract in Matrimony with any Negro or Slave from and after Publication of this Act, That then the said Master Mistress or dame of such free-born woman as aforesaid so married as aforesd shall forfeit and loose all their claim or Title to the Service or Servitude of any such free born woman, and also the said woman Servant so marryed shall and is by this present Act against such Master Mistress or dame (only and no otherwise) absolutely discharged mannumitted and made free instantly upon her Marriage as aforesd from the Service Imployment or demand of any such Master Mistress or dame so offending as afore-said and the said English or white woman to be Servants with their Issues as aforesaid within such marriages...

...the Master Mistress or dame so offending as aforesaid, shall also forfeit the sume of Ten thousand pounds of Tobacco one half to the King and Queen their heirs and Successors for the support of Government within this Province, The other half to him or them that shall informe or sue for the same to be recovered in any Court of Record within this Province by bill plaint or Information wherein no Essoine Protection or wager of Law shall be allowed,

And any Priest Minister Magistrate or other person whatsoever within this Province that shall from and after the Publication hereof joyn in Marriage any Negro or other Slave to any English or other white woman Servant free born as aforesaid shall forfeite and pay the sum of Ten thousand pounds of Tobacco, one half to their said Majesties their heirs and successors, to the use aforesaid and the other half to the Informer to be recovrd as aforesaid Any Law Statute or use-age to the Contrary notwithstanding.

June 4th 1692 June the 2d 1692
Assented to by the Councill Board The house of Assembly
  Signed p Ordr have Assented
  John Llewellin Clk. Signed p Ordr
  Hen: Denton Clk.

<><><>
An Act Relating to Servants & Slaves.

...Provided that any Servant that runs away out of Somersett County into Accomack such person that take him up, shall have but two hundred pounds of Tobacco and no more And whereas some Masters Mistresses and Overseers void of humane pitty & Christian Comisseration have barbarously dismembred and Cauterized their Slaves not only to the Scandall of Christianity, but by such Cruelties keep them from Embracing the same

Be it therefore Enacted by the Authority aforesaid by and with the advice and Consent aforesaid That if any Master Mistress or overseer with the privity consent or procurement of such Master or Mistress as aforesaid, shall after this Act dismember or Cauterize any such Slave, it shall be lawfull for the Justices of the County Court upon proof thereof to manu-mitt and set free such slave to all intents and purposses what-soever....

...And in case any Master Mistress or overseer with the knowledge and consent of such Master or Mistress as afore mentioned shall deny suffict meat drink Lodging and Cloathing or shall unreasonably burthen them beyond their strength with labour or deny them necessary rest and sleep, be it to any English Servant or Slave, It shall be lawfull in such Cases upon due proof thereof to the Justices of the County Court for the first & second Offence, to Fine the said Master Mistress or overseer as to them shall seem meet,

and for the third offence to sett them free from their said servitude And whereas Thomas Courtney of St Maries County hath lately most barbarously dismembred and cutt off both the Ears of a certain Mollattoe girl called being a Servant according to a Law of this Province for one and thirty years

Be it therefore further Enacted That the said Mollatoe Girl for the reasons and Causes aforesaid be hereby Manumitted and sett free from her said Master as a recompence for the Injury so of him received as aforesaid

June 4th 1692. June 2d 1692
Assented to by the Councill Board The house of Assembly
Signed p Ordr have Assented
John Llewellin Clk. Signed p Ordr
Hen: Denton Clk.

<><><>

"...By the mid 1600s, the Irish were the main slaves sold to Antigua and Montserrat. At that time, 70% of the total population of Montserrat were Irish slaves..."

"...Ireland quickly became the biggest source of human livestock for English merchants. The majority of the early slaves to the New World were actually white....From 1641 to 1652, over 500,000 Irish were killed by the English and another 300,000 were sold as slaves. Ireland's population fell from about 1,500,000 to 600,000 in one single decade...African slaves were very expensive during the late 1600s (£50 Sterling). Irish slaves came cheap (no more than £5 Sterling)..."..

"...During the 1650s, over 100,000 Irish children between the ages of 10 and 14 were taken from their parents and sold as slaves in the West Indies, Virginia and New England. In this decade, 52,000 Irish (mostly women and children) were sold to Barbados and Virginia. Another 30,000 Irish men and women were also transported and sold to the highest bidder. In 1656, [Oliver] Cromwell ordered that 2000 Irish children be taken to Jamaica and sold as slaves to English settlers."...

"...the African slave trade was just beginning during this same period," ....

"...African slaves, not tainted with the stain of the hated Catholic theology and more expensive to purchase, were often treated far better than their Irish counterparts."...

Excerpts from a disputed article 'The Irish Slave Trade – The Forgotten 'White' Slaves,' 2008 by John Martin of the Montreal-based Center for Research and Globalization

<><><>

The legacy of King James I's proclamation would enslave the Irish in America and the West Indies for 179 years.

Excerpt from: Byrd Jr., H. L. (2016). Proclamation 1625: America's Enslavement of the Irish. United States: FriesenPress, p59.

In this early year of 1625, King James I of England, Scotland, and Ireland proclaimed that all Irish political prisoners be transported and "sold as slaves" to the English planters in the American British colonies and the British West Indies. James saw the transport of Irish as slaves to the colonies as the solution to the problem of "unwanted surplus people" in Ireland and a "shortage of labor" in the colonies. That single act by King James I opened the door to wholesale slavery in the New World.

Excerpt from: Byrd Jr., H. L. (2016). Proclamation 1625: America's Enslavement of the Irish. United States: FriesenPress,

Table 2.1 Shipments of Persons to Virginia by the Virginia Company of London[49]

	1607–10[a]	1610–18[b]	1619–24[c]
Shipped from England	640	1,125	5,009
Survivors in Virginia	65	900	
Total in Virginia, start of period	1,191	5,909	
Alive at end of period	65	600	1,218
Dead en route or in Virginia	575	591	4,691
Death Toll	90%	45%	80%
Annual Death Rate	49.5%	8.2%	26.4%
Death Rate in England	2.5%	2.6%	2.1%

Excerpt from: Byrd Jr., H. L. (2016). Proclamation 1625: America's Enslavement of the Irish. United States: FriesenPress, Pg. 56

The next excerpt from Byrd's *"Proclamation 1625: America's Enslavement of the Irish."* is in reference to the investors of the Virginia Company (Robert Rich, Earl of Warwick) who supported the management of the Virginia Company in "street cleaning" efforts.

Sir Edwin Sandys became treasurer of the Virginia Company and also the colony of Virginia in the New World. He informed the Lord Mayor that he would continue "street cleansing" of children.

In January 1620, a concerned citizen questioned the practice of the collection and distribution of Irish children by force executed by the City of London and the Virginia Company to be used as labor in the colony of Virginia in the New World.

In response to the Londoner's complaint, Sandys wrote King James (Secetary of State Sir Robert Nauton) explaining the practice was an act of humanity as he was selecting the worst children "whom the city is especially desirous to be disburdened". He explained the children would be reformed via the demanding labor offered by slave masters in the colony of Virginia.

The Privy Council of King James responded with praise for "redeeming so many poor souls..." while making them useful to the colony of Virginia.

As a result of this supportive royal response, Irish children lost all legal rights and their parents were unable to keep them. The children were sold for 20 pounds of tobacco in 1620. Female Irish of age were sold for the price of 120 pounds of tobacco . Records show that in 1624, of the 300 children shipped between 1619 and 1622, only 12 were still alive by 1624.

We authorize and require [. . .] the City and the Virginia Company, or any of them, to deliver, receive, and transport into Virginia all and every the foresaid children as shall be most expedient. And if any of them shall be found obstinate to resist or otherwise to disobey such directions as shall be given in this behalf, we do likewise hereby authorize such as shall have the charge of this service to imprison, punish, and dispose any of those children, upon disorder by them or any of them committed, as cause shall require, and so to ship them out for Virginia with as much expedition as may stand with conveniency.[7]

With this Privy Council ruling, the children lost all their legal rights and could be transported to the New World regardless of their desires or that of their parents. These were the children of England, but this decision laid the groundwork for what was to come for the Irish people of Ireland.

Excerpt from: Byrd Jr., H. L. (2016). Proclamation 1625: America's Enslavement of the Irish. United States: FriesenPress, Pg.43

COSMETICS

During Colonial times, cosmetics would be made of such ingredients as rice powder, vinegar, hartshorn (made from deer antlers), gum arabic, and bismuth subnitrate.

One face-paint recipe suggested fermenting lead and vinegar in a pot, resting in horse manure for three weeks until the lead flakes would be ground into a white powder, then mixed with perfume and some dye.

Placing lead on the skin, or in a powder form which can be inhaled, is poisonous. Many socialites of the day actually died from painting their faces with this cosmetic.

Blush or rouge was created by grinding up the red cochineal insect, the same method used to create dye for the British red coats. Other dark ingredients used were safflower, red wine, or sandalwood and others.

But more toxic substances were also used, such as cinnabar, which is mercury sulphide, a toxic substance. Some older reports stated that women who used this as rouge risked blurred vision, kidney damage, losing their teeth and generating excessive saliva. It is doubtful that a toothless drooling woman was the intention of the "image of beauty" which was considered the ideal for colonial times.

Some felt the use of rouge was a status symbol of wealth.

What modern day status symbols do you think might harm your health?

Likewise, eyebrows were colored with a mix of gall-nuts, black lead, frankincense, and myrtle oil.

Some added beauty marks with "patches" of silk which could be placed on the face. In the French court, the location of patches conveyed a message and this trend traveled to other countries.

Some were placed on the dimple to show playfulness. Other patches were positioned on the forehead to be majestic. The corner of the eye denoted passion. So, when introducing politics, a woman who wore a silk beauty patch on the left side of her forehead could have belonged to the Tory party, however those beauty patches on the right indicated support for the Whig party.

These questionable cosmetic ingredients, which in those days caused such adverse health issues, demonstrated the need for an objective group to monitor the cosmetics manufacturing process to ensure they are safe for the wearer.

Today, one such monitoring organization is EWG, the Environmental Working Group, a non-profit organization. The FDA, Food and Drug Administration, also has this responsibility at the Federal Level for the United States of America.

FANS

The language of fans was a quiet way a woman could convey a message without uttering a word. There was no consistent translation for the popular language of fans.which left room for some mistranslations.

The Language of the Fan

Carrying in the right hand in front of face	Follow me
Carrying in the left hand in front of face	Desirous of acquaintance
Placing it on left ear	I wish to get rid of you
Drawing across forehead	You have changed
Twirling in the left hand	We are watched
Carrying in the right hand	You are too willing
Drawing through the hand	I hate you
Twirling in the right hand	I love another
Drawing across the cheek	I love you
Presented shut	Do you love me?
Drawing across the eyes	I am sorry
Touching tip with finger	I wish to speak to you
Letting it rest on right cheek	Yes
Letting it rest on left cheek	No
Open and shut	You are cruel
Dropping it	We will be friends
Fanning slowly	I am married
Fanning quickly	I am engaged
With handle to lips	Kiss me
Open wide	Wait for me
Carrying in left hand, open	Come and talk to me
Placed behind head	Don't forget me
With little finger extended	Good-bye

Fan Flirtations.

Carrying in right hand in front of face.............*Follow me.*
Carrying in left hand ....*Desirous of an acquaintance.*
Placing it on the right ear....................*You have changed.*
Twirling it in left hand ....*I wish to get rid of you.*
Drawing across forehead ....*We are watched.*
Carrying in right hand ....*You are too willing.*
Drawing through the hand ....*I hate you.*
Twirling in right hand.......................*I love another.*
Drawing across the cheek.......................*I love you.*
Closing it ....*I wish to speak to you.*
Drawing across the eye.......................*I am sorry*

Letting it rest on right cheek............................*Yes.*
Letting it rest on left cheek............................*No.*
Open and shut ....*You are cruel.*
Dropping............................*We will be friends.*
Fanning slow ....*I am married.*
Fanning fast ....*I am engaged.*
With handle to lips............................*Kiss me.*
Shut............................*You have changed.*
Open wide ....*Wait for me.*

Victorian fan etiquette from *Cassell's Magazine*, 1866

1. A fan placed near the heart: "You have won my love."

2. A closed fan touching the right eye: "When may I be allowed to see you?"

3. The number of sticks shown answered the question: "At what hour?"

4. Threatening gestures with a closed fan: "Do not be so imprudent"

5. Half-opened fan pressed to the lips: "You may kiss me."

6. Hands clasped together holding an open fan: "Forgive me."

7. Covering the left ear with an open fan: "Do not betray our secret."

8. Hiding the eyes behind an open fan: "I love you."

9. Shutting a fully-opened fan slowly: "I promise to marry you."

10. Drawing the fan across the eyes: "I am sorry."

11. Touching the finger to the tip of the fan: "I wish to speak with you."

12. Letting the fan rest on the right cheek: "Yes."

13. Letting the fan rest on the left cheek: "No."

14. Opening and closing the fan several times: "You are cruel"

15. Dropping the fan: "We will be friends."

16. Fanning slowly: "I am married."

17. Fanning quickly: "I am engaged."

18. Putting the fan handle to the lips: "Kiss me."

19. Opening a fan wide: "Wait for me."

20. Placing the fan behind the head: "Do not forget me"

21. Placing the fan behind the head with finger extended: "Goodbye."

22. Fan in right hand in front of face: "Follow me."

23. Fan in left hand in front of face: "I am desirous of your acquaintance."

24. Fan held over left ear: "I wish to get rid of you."

25. Drawing the fan across the forehead: "You have changed."

26. Twirling the fan in the left hand: "We are being watched."

27. Twirling the fan in the right hand: "I love another."

28. Carrying the open fan in the right hand: "You are too willing."

29. Carrying the open fan in the left hand: "Come and talk to me."

30. Drawing the fan through the hand: "I hate you!"

31. Drawing the fan across the cheek: "I love you!"

32. Presenting the fan shut: "Do you love me?"

14 Vocabulary

In the early 1770s, before the colonies united into the United States of America, some words and terms were used, which may be explained in this section.

almanac: A reference book with calendars, lists, charts, etc.

compliant: Ready to agree. Yielding.

encounter: To meet.

non-verbal: Not using written or spoken words. Using gestures and facial expressions, instead.

perplexed: Confused. Puzzled.

perturbed: Upset, worried, troubled.

succumb: To give up. To be defeated.

ABOUT Wynter Sommers

Wynter Sommers is the pseudonym for an American writing team, which harnesses multiple skills in technology, research, history and education. Formally trained with a PhD in Education, Wynter Sommers blends academic classroom experience, with corporate sophistication, and a passion for developing more effective student insights through engaging storytelling. Wynter Sommers has a heart to inspire creativity and develop critical thinking skills, all to encourage readers to make wise choices in life.

Wynter Sommers takes each story and weaves the plot with classic gripping elements, which endure throughout repeated readings, revealing new meanings each time the story is explored. The small choices a reader makes in real life could have a lasting effect in future generations. This set of stories shows the origin of not just Bjorn Esterday and Sarah Paradise, but of their ancestors and the sort of world which was established, which unfolded in each generation until Bjorn and Sarah met.

It is rewarding to learn of heartfelt, thought provoking conversations taking place globally about the characters of these books. Should the reader be presented with extraordinary circumstances, it is the sincerest wish that they act with honor, truth and integrity to overcome obstacles in real life whilst the reader hones skills of self-reliance and collaborative teamwork despite barriers outside of the reader's control. Wynter Sommers hopes you enjoy the other *Bjorn Esterday Was not Born Yesterday* stories in this series.